The Legend: Tournament

Part I

By: RJ Walker

Chapter 1

Mack was suiting up in North Forest's visitor's locker room for the final district game before the North Forest Invitational. The gym was finished in the first week of June, and the tournament started a month later. Today, Mack and the Wolves were about to face the other toughest team in the district, the North Forest Knights, the tournament hosts. The Wolves had beaten them both times prior, once in preseason and once during the regular season, but it was a battle both times. Mack finished putting on his uniform, complete with his new Kyrie 4's, courtesy of Mr. Joe Livingston, head scout for the Duke Blue Devils basketball team. He put on his shooting shirt, and walked through the locker room, watching the rest of his teammates put the finishing touches on their uniforms. He headed out of the locker room into the gym and was greeted by a chorus of cheers. He was the top high school basketball prospect in the country, and almost every game that he played in sold out. He went and grabbed a basketball out of the rack by the door and stepped out onto the shiny new court to warm up.

About half an hour after the rest of the team came out of the locker room to warm up, the head referee blew his whistle and called the two captains out to center court. Mack walked out to the giant Knight in the middle of the floor, and met his gametime matchup, King Gomez. King Gomez was the second-best high school player in the country, based on ESPN's rankings. The only player better than him was Mack, and Mack's best friend, Miles, was a close third in the rankings. Mack and King shook hands at midcourt and went back to their huddles. When Mack got back, Coach White called out the starters to begin the game, and they went out onto the court. Both teams bumped fists with each other, the ball went up into the air, and the game began. Jackson, the Wolves' starting center, tipped the ball back to Miles, and he walked it up the court. When Miles got the ball to center court, he burst into action. He put the ball between his legs and behind his back, then drove to the goal from the left wing. He faked like he was going to lay the ball up, but he passed the ball to Johnny, at the last second, in the corner. Johnny executed a perfect pump-fake, and drove on the baseline, putting up a floater that dropped right through the net. On the next possession, Mack brought the ball up the floor after a three-point miss by King. He faked left and drove right, banking in a running teardrop off the back of the glass. King caught the inbound, and jogged the ball up the court, directing his teammates to the right positions on the floor. He crossed midcourt and was immediately swarmed by Mack and Miles. He tried to dribble behind his back, but did it too loosely, and

Miles stole the ball. Mack took off down the court, with Miles on his left. Miles threw the ball ahead to Mack, but when he went up for a layup, it was blocked from behind by King. Miles caught the ball in the right corner before it went out of bounds and shot a short midrange jumper that pushed the score to 6-0. King grabbed the inbound, pushed the ball down court, and scored a layup to make it

a four-point deficit. Miles brought
the ball up the court and passed it
to Mack so he could set up the
offense. He passed the ball to
Johnny and cut toward the basket.
Johnny passed the ball back to him
when he beat King to the basket.
Mack caught the ball, faked a
layup, and spun around to throw an
alley-oop to Jackson, who caught it
and dunked it home. King caught
the inbound, and Mack was right

on his tail the entire time dribbling up the court. Once King crossed halfcourt, he turned on the jets and raced to the cup, leaving an off-guard Mack in the dust. He jumped into the air and made a double-clutch layup to bring the score back within four points, 8-4. Mack brought the ball up the court and set up the offense. He passed the ball to David, who had just come off a v-cut. Mack then set a screen for Miles, who faked a cut, and ran

back to the top of the three-point

line, wide open. David passed him

the ball and he shot a three, hitting

nothing but net. King brought the

ball back up the court, faked left,

and drove right to the basket. Mack

stayed with him the whole time,

and when King jumped for a layup,

Mack smacked it right into the

hands of Miles. Miles took off, with

his opponent guarding him closely

all the way up the court. When
Miles got to the basket, he jumped
in the air to make a layup, and the
Knight's point guard jumped at the
same time. Miles hung in the air
and twisted his body to the left side
of the goal and made a left-handed
layup as the referee blew his
whistle, signaling a shooting foul.
The crowd cheered as Miles got up
from the floor and high-fived his
teammates. He walked to the free

throw line and knocked down the free throw to give the Wolves a 10-point lead.

At the beginning of the 2nd quarter, the Wolves kept a 12-point lead, 24-12. Mack and Miles piled up most of those points, Mack scoring 9, and Miles scoring 10. The Wolves got the first possession of the 2nd quarter, and Mack caught the inbound from Jackson. He walked the ball up the court, but when he crossed halfcourt, he

sprang into action. He put the ball

behind his back and cross-stepped

into a shot hesitation. He put the

ball over one arm to sell the "hesi"

(hesitation in basketball lingo),

then spun on his pivot foot and

landed on both feet in perfect

shooting form. He shot the ball,

and the crowd cheered as it

dropped through the net. Mack ran

back on defense and stole the ball

from King when he crossed half

court. He grabbed the ball and

raced down the court, with King

right on his heels. He knew that

Jackson was running down the

court behind King, so when he got

to the goal, he threw the ball

against the backboard and ran off

the court. King jumped to catch the

ball, and when he did, Jackson

came in from behind and slammed

it home, over his head. The crowd

cheered even louder when he made the dunk, and it became pandemonium when Mack stole the inbound and slammed down a vicious dunk, roaring with adrenaline. The Knights' coach called a timeout, and the crowd exploded. Coach White told his players to stay on the court, and soon enough, play resumed. King brought the ball up the floor and drove to the left towards the goal.

As he was dribbling toward the
goal, he didn't notice Johnny
coming over from the weak side.
So, when he went to pick the ball
up, he got stripped. Johnny grabbed
the ball and yanked it away from
King, then threw it backwards over
his head to a streaking Miles, who
finished with a left-handed
underhand layup. The next
possession, Mack brought the ball
up the court after a North Forest

miss and stopped about 3 feet away

from the three-point line. He

accidentally picked up the ball, so

he was stuck. King rushed forward

to prevent a pass, but Mack

anticipated that. He jumped into

the air, leaned into King's body,

and shot the long three. The ref

blew the whistle, signaling for a

foul, and the ball sailed through the

air. It banked into the net off the

backboard, and Mack pumped his

fist. He walked up to the free throw

line and shot the extra shot but

missed. Luckily, Jackson caught the

rebound and put the ball back into

the goal with one hand. King

brought the ball up the floor and

attacked the basket with brute

force. He backed Mack down

towards the goal, and spun towards

the middle of the paint, where

Jackson was waiting for him. King

jumped towards the goal and

tossed up a short floater that floated right over Jackson's fingertips and dropped through the net. Miles brought the ball up the court and passed it to David. He dribbled to the top of the three-point line, called the key, and set up the offense, putting everyone into position. He passed the ball to Mack on the right wing and cut through the lane towards the basket. Mack tossed him an "alley-oop", and he caught it with both hands and dunked it. The Wolves got back down the court to play defense, and the crowd cheered when King tried to pass the ball, and it got intercepted by Mack halfway to its target. Mack took off down the court with King chasing him down. King caught him at the free throw line and grabbed his shoulders to prevent a layup. Mack tossed the ball up towards the goal as the whistle blew and roared with

adrenaline when the ball went

through the net. Miles ran down

the court and high-fived him, then

he walked to the free throw line. He

shot the free throw, but it bounced

off the back of the rim. King caught

the rebound and raced in front of

the rest of the pack. Mack chased

him down the court, and when he

went up for a layup, Mack smacked

the ball out of bounds. The Knights

inbounded the ball, and the point guard caught it. He drove to the left, but Jackson smacked the ball out of his hands, to the middle of the court. Mack and King raced to midcourt, and both of them dove on the floor for the ball. They grabbed the ball at the same time and tried to pull it away from each other. The referee blew the whistle and signaled for a jump ball. Mack and King lined up to jump, and the referee threw the ball into the air.

Mack tapped the ball backwards to

David, who threw a football pass to

Miles, who was streaking down the

left sideline. He caught the ball,

and tossed it behind him into the

air, where Mack was waiting to

catch it and dunk it home. David

held his arms up in the air to signal

a touchdown, and the Knights

coach called a timeout. Mack and

the Wolves jogged to the bench,

energized by the power play by Mack, Miles, and David. They had pushed the score to 44-14, with one minute left in the second quarter.

King brought the ball up the court on the next possession, ready to try and get this crowd back on the Knights' side. He drove towards the basket and threw up a wild shot that hit the back of the rim and bounced out of bounds. Mack quickly grabbed the ball and passed the inbound to Miles, who took off up the court. He called for a screen from David, and when he obliged, Miles drove to the right and popped out to the corner. He crossed his defender with some fancy dribble moves that he had practiced at the Rec and drove baseline and dropped in a left-handed floater. The Knights point guard brought the ball up the court and passed it to

King, who drove and went for a

slam, but was blocked from behind

by Jackson. Mack picked up the ball

and threw it a three-quarter court

pass to an outletting Miles, who

laid the ball up as time expired in

the first half. The crowd cheered as

The Wolves jogged off the court,

holding a 48-14 lead.

Chapter 2

When the 3rd quarter was
about to begin, the Wolves jogged
out of the locker room to the bench.
North Forest jogged out of the
locker room across the court, their
starters wearing warm-up clothes,
and their bench players ready to
start the half. The ref blew his
whistle, and the half began. Miles
brought the ball up the court, and
passed it to David, who swung the

ball across the court to Mack. Mack pump faked in the corner, drove down the baseline, bumped his defender to make room, and scored a right-handed layup. Mack jogged back on defense and started guarding North Forest's bench small forward once he crossed half court. The Knight's point guard tried to throw a pass inside to his center, but Jackson deflected it right into Miles' waiting hands.

Miles raced down the court, David

in tow, and tossed the ball off the

backboard. The defender between

Miles and David jumped for the

ball, but David slammed it home

over his head, bodying him into the

wall behind the basket. David

dropped down from the rim and

flexed on the defender, then ran

back on defense. Mack grabbed the

rebound off of a missed shot by

North Forest and raced down the

court in front of the pack, bounced

the ball hard off the floor, and

slammed home a reverse dunk. He

jumped down from the rim,

pumped his fists at the crowd, and

yelled as the Knights called a

timeout.

After the timeout, the Wolves

came back out onto the court

looking better than ever. Miles

stole the Knights' inbound and

tossed it behind his back to Johnny,

who shot a three from the halfcourt

logo, making nothing but net. The

Knights scored a quick basket, and

Mack caught the inbound from

David. He crossed halfcourt and ran

a high screen and roll with Jackson.

Jackson set the screen, then rolled

to the basket. Mack faked the one-

handed pass and did a quick in-

and-out dribble before driving

down the left side of the paint and

scoring a slick left-handed layup, virtually unguarded. King had been quiet the whole game, with only 5 points on 2-9 shooting, which is the main reason the Knights were losing. He brought the ball up the court, and after a quick double cross that stunned Mack, he ran down the middle of the lane and tossed up a floater with Jackson in front of him. Jackson jumped up and swatted back King's floater

right into Mack's hands. Mack
tossed a halfcourt look away pass
to Miles, who threw down a rare
slam dunk. The Knights brought
the ball down the court with 15
seconds left, and King had the ball.
He called an isolation play and got
Mack on the right wing. He called
for a screen and David came up and
switched onto King. King crossed
him over with 3 seconds left, and
took him straight to the goal,

where he made a slick reverse layup with half a second left, one of the few bright spots for the Knights. Jackson took the ball out of bounds and rolled the inbound to Mack, who let it roll to halfcourt before picking the ball up and launching a halfcourt shot that airballed, ending the quarter.

After the game, Mack and the rest of the Wolves headed to the locker room to discuss the game and their plans for the night. "I'm just going to head home and get some rest. I'm exhausted," said Mack, grabbing clothes to change into. "Dang it, I have trumpet sectionals today, or I'd walk with you," Miles said, grabbing his bag from his locker. "I have to help my dad with the bar tonight, he has a big party coming from New England. I'm on my way now if any of you want to come." Mack headed toward the door and told Johnny, "I might make a quick run-through on my way home," and walked out of the locker room.

Chapter 3

Mack was on his way home when a large black SUV pulled up beside him, and the right rear window rolled down. Mack looked over, and the culprit was none other than Luke Alan, the head basketball recruiter for North Carolina. "Need a ride?" said Mr. Alan, pushing open the door to the Cadillac. "Sure, why not?" said Mack, climbing in next to Mr. Alan.

"Any place in particular?" said Luke, pulling the door closed.

"Yup, The Teen Bar on the corner of 49th," Mack said. Luke Alan's driver took off, slowly picking up speed as they drove down the street. "So, Mack, do you have any idea why I'm in Boston? asked Mr. Alan, pulling a water bottle out of his minifridge in the backseat. "I suspect it's to watch me play," said Mack, as he tried to get comfortable in his seat. "Yes, it is. I heard you got an offer from Duke a few weeks ago and wanted to see what all the hype was about. One of the largest basketball schools in the country offering a freshman a full ride is a big deal. Now I know why. They were smart to nab you early. Your confidence and swagger on the court is unmatched by any high schooler I've seen this season, and I've gotten around a bit." As they pulled up in front of the teen

bar, Mr. Alan got to the point.

Handing Mack an envelope, he

said, "Mack, I'd like to make you a

formal offer for a full scholarship

from the University of North

Carolina. I think we can harness

your talents and make you the

most skilled player in the country."

Mack took the envelope and said, "I

really appreciate the offer Mr. Alan,

but I've got three years to think

about college, right now I just want to focus on basketball." "Alright, I understand where you're coming from Mack, I know it must be a lot to digest right now. Just call and ask me if you have any questions or need a favor," said Mr. Alan, handing Mack a business card as he got out of the car in front of the teen bar. "Thanks for the ride, Mr. Alan," Mack said, closing the door.

He waited until the car drove off and walked to the door, and as he went to open it, he saw a party of teenage girls about his age walking from a car, laughing and talking. In the lead was Jasmine Cole, the star point guard for North Forest. Last year she was the district Female Athlete of the Year, after leading her team to a nearly undefeated season, losing only one game to Hillmore in the regular season. She got her revenge in the championship, scoring 33 and leading her team to the district title. She was pretty, smart, and a very good basketball player. Currently walking toward the teen bar, she seemed to be enjoying herself, but something in her body language told Mack that she would rather be anywhere else. Mack waited for them to get close, then held the door for them as they all

walked through. "Thanks,"
Jasmine said, walking through last.
After giving a second glance to the
gentleman holding the door, she
said, "Hey, aren't you Mack
Williams?" "Yup, that's me," said
Mack, walking in behind her.
"Maybe I'll catch you later?" he
said, heading toward the restroom.
"Maybe," Jasmine responded,
heading towards her friends at the
bar. Mack came back from the

restroom and found his friends sitting in a corner booth next to a window. Mack took the edge seat next to Miles, and said, "Did you guys see Jasmine Cole over there at the bar? She looks like she doesn't want to be here." Miles responded, "I know that look, that's the face you have when you have a bad game and want to be in the gym. Maybe you should go and see what's wrong with her. "Ok, I'll be right back," Mack said, getting up from the table. He walked toward the bar, but Jasmine was nowhere to be found. "She was just here," he thought. He turned around to head back to his table, and ran right into Jasmine, coming back from the bathroom. "Oh, sorry," said Mack. "I was just looking for you." "Was there a specific reason you were looking for me?" Jasmine said, stepping back. "I was actually coming to see if you wanted to go somewhere with me." "And where is it that you want me to go with you?" Jasmine asked, smirking. "A court," Mack said, pointing to his basketball shoes hanging from his backpack. "I was looking for someone to shoot around with, and who better than the Female Athlete of the Year." Jasmine laughed and said, "I'll call my mom and ask, but it should be a yes. I don't have

my shoes with me though." "I have
a car now, we can go by your house
on the way," Mack said, dangling
his keys. "Ok, I'll see you in a sec,"
Jasmine said, pulling out her phone
and dialing. Mack headed to the
parking lot to grab his car, when he
remembered that he had gotten a
ride from Mr. Alan, and that his car
was still at the school. He turned
around to go back inside, but
Jasmine walked through the door at

that moment, and said, "My mom said we could go, but I have to be home by midnight." She looked around the parking lot, and asked, "Where's your car?" "Funny story," Mack said, looking back at the parking lot. "I got a ride from Mr. Alan, a scout from North Carolina, and left my car in the school parking lot. I can walk back and get it, and pick you up, or you can walk with me." "I'll walk with you," said Jasmine, slipping her phone into her pocket. "It's only like a 20-minute walk, we passed the school on the way here."

"Alright then, let's get moving," Mack said, moving toward the parking lot, and soon joined by Jasmine, made his way down the street toward the school.

Chapter 4

When Mack and Jasmine got
to the school, Mack walked over to
his Ram 1500 truck and unlocked
the door, letting Jasmine get in the
passenger side first. "So, what
neighborhood do you live in?"
asked Mack, starting the truck and
shifting into reverse. "I live in
Celtic Spring," said Jasmine,
putting on her seatbelt. "Ok, your
neighborhood is on the way. We'll

go to my house first so I can grab my shorts, then hit your house on the way to the court," said Mack, pulling out of the parking lot. "Sounds like a plan," said Jasmine, leaning back in her seat. "So, tell me Mack, why is a big celebrity like you at the teen bar right after a game? Don't you have interviews and shoe deals?" Jasmine asked, giggling. Mack laughed and said, "Your sarcasm is not lost on me, but since we won, there weren't nearly as many interviews tonight. You should see me after a loss, I don't even get a shower until 2 hours after the game." Mack and Jasmine continued talking and laughing until they pulled onto Mack's street. Mack parked in the driveway of his house and said, "I'll be right back, I'm going to grab shorts and water. I'll be right back." He hopped out of the car and ran into the house, only to return a split second later without water or a pair of shorts. "I totally forgot that I keep a spare gym bag with workout stuff in the car under the seat," Mack said, lifting the back seat to reveal a bag of gym clothes. "If you want, you can wear these shorts and I can grab some from the house, that way we'll have more time at the court." "If they're clean, I'll wear them," Jasmine said, laughing. "Alright, then I'll be right back," Mack said, smirking. He ran back into the house and came back a short time later with another pair of gym shorts and a basketball. "Ready to go?" he asked, opening the door of the truck, and climbing inside. "Always," Jasmine said, putting her seatbelt back on.

They were in a deep conversation about whether pineapple belongs on pizza, when Mack pulled his truck into the parking lot of what looked like an old, abandoned barn. "I'm telling you, don't knock it until you try it," he said, hopping out of the car and changing into shorts. "Yeah sure, it probably tastes like spicy fruit on bread," Jasmine said, getting out on the passenger side.

"Where are we anyway?" she asked. "I'VE DRIVEN YOU TO YOUR DOOOOM," said Mack, holding a flashlight in front of him. "Just kidding, but it is a pretty cool place. Take the ball and head on in, the lights are on the right when you walk in." "Fine, but don't scare me like that," Jasmine said, smirking slyly at Mack before grabbing the ball and heading inside. Mack tossed his things into the truck, locked it, and followed her inside.

The warehouse was way bigger on the inside than it looked from the outside. Jasmine flicked on the fluorescent lights just as Mack yanked open the barn door. She was blinded by the light, and when she got her sight back, she was amazed. The barn had been transformed into a full-sized court, complete with basketball racks,

bleachers, and regulation hoops.

Mack walked by and smiled,

saying, "My Dad helped me fix this

place up a few years ago, in 7th

grade. I told him that I was going

to get serious about basketball, so

he told me to prove it, and this is

how I did it. The only people that

have been in here are my parents,

and Miles, and now, you. I don't

really like to broadcast it because

everyone would want to come and play here. I hope you'll respect that." "Of course, I won't tell anyone," Jasmine said. "This is the coolest thing I've ever seen. I can't wait to beat you on your own court." Mack laughed and said, "Bring it, let's see what you got." "I'll definitely bring it here, this is the point of no return," Jasmine said, tossing him the ball.

They played until they were both drenched in sweat, and they decided to head home for the night. Mack and Jasmine both hopped into his truck after locking up the gym. "I had fun tonight, kicking your butt," Jasmine said, on the ride back to her house. "I had fun too, even though I lost quite a bit, I didn't know you had that deep of a bag. I'm definitely going to use some of your tricks in my next game. I might as well see what happens," Mack replied, pulling up to Jasmine's house. "I'll see you around Mack," Jasmine said, pushing open the truck door and getting out of the truck. "Alright, I'll see you." Mack waited until Jasmine locked herself in the house before pulling off down the street toward his home.

The next morning, Mack woke up with a splitting headache.

He tried to sit up but couldn't. He called his mom into his room, and she checked his temperature. "I could make you go to school today, but I don't want this to turn into something worse, so I'm going to let you stay home today," Mack's mom said. "Your Dad and I have to work today, so as long as you are ready to go to school tomorrow, you can hang out here. Just make sure to drink lots of water to bring that headache down." "Ok, thanks Mom," said Mack, rolling over and dozing off. His mom turned his light out and left the room to get ready for work.

When Mack woke up later, the house was totally silent. He got up and went to the restroom, brushed his teeth, and washed his face. He then changed into some workout clothes and went for a run.

He sprinted all the way down his
street and jogged through the rest
of his neighborhood. When he came
back to the house, Miles was
outside shooting hoops. "Want to
come over and shoot hoops?" asked
Miles, hitting a fadeaway jumper.

"I can't," said Mack. "I'm
supposed to be resting because I
woke up sick, and I thought a run
would help clear my mind. I feel a
little better now, but I'm going to

go inside and hop in the shower."

"Alright man, rest up, because we need you for the game this week," replied Miles, laying the ball up. "Definitely, I'll catch you later." Mack continued on his run until he made it to his front door. He headed inside, locked the door, and got ready to get in the shower when he got a FaceTime call from Jasmine. "Hey," she said, staring at Mack's abs. "Hey yourself," he replied. "I was just about to hop in the shower, but what's up?" "I was wondering if you wanted to go and get some shots up at your indoor warehouse court," she said, finally diverting her eyes from his abs and looking at him. "I'm technically supposed to be resting, but I guess I can drive you over there and watch, I don't think I'm going to play," Mack said, grabbing his truck keys. "I can be there in 15 minutes; will you be ready?" "I'll be ready, 15 minutes is plenty of time." "Ok then, I'll see you in a few," Mack said, hanging up the phone. He pulled his shirt back on, put on his crocs, and hopped into his truck, taking off in a heartbeat towards Jasmine's house.

Chapter 5

When Mack and Jasmine arrived at the warehouse, there was no one in sight. They got out of the truck and headed over to the door, where Mack unlocked the door and followed Jasmine inside. He grabbed a ball and tossed it over to her, where she took a rhythm jump shot from the right elbow. Mack watched her shoot around for a few minutes, then grabbed a ball and started shooting on a side goal. He ran and grabbed the ball from the other side of the court after a miss, and suddenly had a rush of adrenaline. Mack ran full speed at the rim, jumped, and dunked it home. Everything would have been fine if he hadn't lost his grip on the rim. His fingers slipped and he fell face first toward the ground, and he used his right forearm, his shooting arm, to try and break his fall. There was a sharp pain in his wrist as soon as he landed, and he knew that something was wrong. He yelled in pain and Jasmine ran over. "What happened?" she asked anxiously, examining his wrist. "I slipped off the rim after I dunked and landed on my wrist." His arm had immediately started to swell up, and it was a bluish-purple color. When Jasmine went to touch it, Mack flinched so hard he almost fell backwards. "We need to get you to the hospital, now," she said, helping him stand. "We have to get that wrist checked out asap, but I'm pretty sure you fractured it." They made it outside, and Jasmine locked up the warehouse. They hurried over to the truck, and she was on her way to the passenger seat when she realized that Mack couldn't drive. "Mack, give me your keys, you can't even drive in this condition." "Mack grunted in agreement and pulled the keys from his pocket, tossing them to Jasmine. She grabbed them, started the truck, and drove towards the hospital.

When they arrived at the hospital, Mack was taken straight back to a room where a doctor came to examine his wrist, and ultimately confirmed that his wrist was fractured. "You'll be out 6–8 weeks, as it stands now. As long as you don't reaggravate it, you should be ready to roll in a month and a half." "Thanks Doc, but are you sure there's no way I can be back faster? The North Forest Summer Invitational starts in two weeks, and I want to play," says Mack, looking disappointed. "The only way it will heal any faster is if it's actually a hairline fracture, because in that case, it will only take a week to heal, considering how bad it is. I can run another MRI if you want me to," the doctor responded. "Yes, please, anything to make the healing process speed up."

After the MRI, the doctor came back with the results, saying that it was, 'by God's will alone', a sprain and not a fracture. It was only going to take a week to heal

after all. Mack looked pleased after

getting his wrist taped up by the

nurse. He thanked the nurses and

doctor and headed back out to the

waiting room where Jasmine was

waiting. "You look pretty happy for

someone who just fractured their

wrist," she said, pulling his arm

closer so she could get a better

look. "The doctor said it was a

sprain, not a fracture, and that I

would be good to go in a week,
right on time to play in the
tournament. I still don't even feel
well, I knew I should've stayed
sitting instead of trying to dunk,"
Mack responded, heading for the
door. "You technically should have
been at home, and that's my fault. I
asked you to take me when I
could've gone to a local gym,"
Jasmine said. "It's alright, I think
I'm ready to go home now

though," Mack said, laughing. He opened the door of the front passenger seat, and a moment later, Jasmine got into the driver's seat.

As Jasmine drove toward her house, she asked Mack what made him want to pursue basketball. "Well," he said, "I was always a very fast kid, I used to win races by a mile because of my first step and speed. I was always decent at basketball, but once I learned how to combine that first step with my dribbling and athleticism, it just became a matter of working on my shooting and finishing ability."

"Oh ok," Jasmine said, "that makes sense." They rode in silence until they got to Jasmine's house, but when she went to get out of the truck, Mack said, "Wait, I have to ask you something. Do you even have a driver's license?" Jasmine

laughed and said, "Nope, I'm

taking the Driver's Ed course now

though, so I'll have it by winter.

Goodnight Mack, I'll call you in the

morning to see how your wrist is

doing." "Ok, goodnight," Mack

said, watching her get out of the

car and head inside.

Chapter 6

When Mack got into the house, his mom was sitting in the living room watching TV. When she saw his hand bound up in a cast, she gasped and exclaimed, "What happened?" "I fell on it while I was shooting around at the barn. Jasmine helped get me to the hospital and the doctor said that I'll be fine in a week." Mack's mom got up and examined his cast, sending him on his way after she gave it a stern once-over. He left the living room, and went to his room, where he sat on the bed and stared at the cast.

Fifteen minutes later, he finally got up and got in the shower. He had to put a large plastic bag over his hand to keep the cast from getting wet. After his shower, he put on a muscle shirt and shorts and hopped in bed. He lay there for a while, gathering his thoughts. Mack decided that if he was going to come back as the player he was before the injury, he would have to keep his strength and conditioning above par. When his dad returned home from his nightly walk, he went to see Mack, but he was already fast asleep.

When Mack woke up the next morning, his left side of his face was killing him. He sat up and

realized that he had been laying on

his cast all night, and that it had

left imprints along his cheek and

neck. He hopped out of the bed,

took a shower, threw on some

clothes, and was on his way out the

door within 15 minutes. He saw

Miles making his way over to

Mack's driveway, where he would

drive them both to school. As soon

as Miles saw the cast on Mack's

arm, his eyes went wide. "What happened, dude?" he asked, grabbing Mack's arm to get a better look. "I had a little accident at the barn," Mack said, pulling his arm away. "I was there shooting with Jasmine last night, and I fell after dunking. She drove me to the hospital and waited with me while I got the cast on. Now that I've told the story again, can we please just go to school and act like nothing happened?" So that's what they did. When they arrived at school, and people started to notice the cast on Mack's arm, he and Miles had to tell the story countless times to students and teachers. Finally came the end of the day, and practice. When Mack went into the locker room, the entire team crowded around him and asked what had happened. He pushed his way through the crowd, ignoring them all, and went into Coach White's office. "Coach, I sprained my wrist last night practicing. I went up for a dunk, slipped off the rim, and came down hard on my arm. The doctor said I'll be out for a week, but I should be ready for the summer tournament." Coach White took a long look at the cast and said, "Normally, I'd be frantic, but I think our team is good enough not to lose another game the rest of the season, even with

you out. I want you to rest that arm

but come to practice and watch.

And help whenever you can. That's

the only way the players will have

the confidence to keep this train

rolling. I'll also expect you to sit on

the bench during the games, cheer

on the team, and give any feedback

you have during timeouts. Just

because you can't play doesn't

mean you're not a huge part of this

team." "I understand Coach, I'll do whatever I can to help the team win, even from the bench. I'll go change and I can run laps and stretch with them to keep my strength and cardio up." Mack opened the door to his Coach's office and was greeted by the other guys from the team. "Miles told us what happened, and we're going to be here to support you in any way that we can until you're healthy," said David, giving Mack a fist bump. Mack turned to the team and said, "I appreciate that guys. But the biggest way you guys can help me is by winning the rest of the season. I don't want to come back and have to fight my way through the tournament. I want to be a top seed, and slowly gain my rhythm by playing weaker teams in the beginning, because I still want to win this tournament. I'll workout with you guys, and be on the bench every game, but you guys are going to have to play hard and controlled, just like we do. That's the only way that we can do what we want to do." Mack headed toward his locker to change, and inside, was a note from Jasmine. "Come out by the water fountains. It'll only take a few seconds." Mack changed quickly and jogged out to the water fountains, where Jasmine was waiting. "How did you get in here?" Mack asked, smirking. "No one questioned me when I walked in through the football doors, so I just made my way back here. I knew where it was because my sister went here when I was in middle school." "Ok, so what's up? Practice is about to start, and I promised I'd do whatever I could to be there for the team." "I really just wanted to apologize," said

Jasmine. "I should've let you rest yesterday instead of going to shoot with you. I feel really bad about it, so I want to take you out to dinner this weekend. We can eat whatever you want, the only condition is, you'll either have to drive or let me drive your truck." Mack thought for a moment, and said, "I'll text you where I want to eat when practice is over." "Perfect, it's a date," Jasmine said, hugging Mack quickly and jogging back the way she came,

right out the football facility doors.

Mack turned to go into the gym,

but caught Johnny and David

peeking around a corner, watching.

"Oooooooo, Mack has a girlfriend,"

they teased, as he laughed and

punched them both lightly in the

arm. "C'mon fellas," he said. "We

have games to win."

After practice, Mack texted Jasmine on his way to his truck. "I like The Teen Bar for dinner this weekend, I don't want to run your pockets thin." She replied, "That's cool with me, pick me up at 8 on Saturday, and we'll grab that."

"Sounds like a plan," Mack texted, then he got in his truck with Miles so they could head home.

Chapter 7

On Saturday night, Mack put on some nice jeans and a polo shirt, hopped in his truck, and went to get Jasmine. He arrived at her house about 5 minutes before 8. He went up to the door, rang the doorbell, and waited. He waited for about a minute until finally, Jasmine's mother answered the door. "Hi, you must be Mack," she

said, opening the door wider.
"Come on in, Jasmine's just
finishing up." "Thank you," Mack
said, following her inside. When he
arrived in the living room, he saw
toys strewn about everywhere, and
heard laughing from a large
bedroom that was off to the side.
"Hey, come out of there you little
rascals," Jasmine's mom said,
walking towards the room. She
came back after about 30 seconds,

holding two small children, twins. The boys jumped out of her arms as soon as she made it back to the living room and started playing with the trucks and cars on the floor. "As you can see, I stay very busy," she said, laughing.

"Jasmine's dad is on a business trip for a few days, so I'm left here with the boys until he gets back." "I like that. I always wished I had a younger brother," Mack said, tousling the closest twin's hair.

"My teammate Miles is the closest

thing I have to a brother, we've

known each other since 3rd grade,

and we do almost everything

together." Right as Mack finished

telling Jasmine's mom a story

about an AAU tournament that he

and Miles had in 7th grade,

Jasmine herself came down the

stairs. "Mack, I'm really sorry. I

lost track of time, and before I

knew it, it was 7:45. We can go another day if you have to get home, I know it's about 8:30, and we haven't left yet." "No, it's ok, I was actually having a great conversation with your mom and meeting your brothers. We can go tonight because I still haven't eaten," Mack said, laughing and standing up. It was really nice to meet you, Mrs. Cole, I'll bring Jasmine home safely." "I'm sure you will Mack, you two have a good time," Mrs. Cole said, walking them to the door. As Mack and Jasmine headed to the truck, Mack said, "Your mom is a really nice lady, and she's relatable." "Yeah, that's what all my teammates say about her," Jasmine said. "Do you want me to drive, because of your wrist?" "No, you're paying for dinner, the least I can do is drive, even with this busted wrist." They hopped in the truck, Mack honked a goodbye, and they took off towards The Teen bar. "It's a good thing the bar doesn't close until 2 am, because I'm pretty hungry," Jasmine joked. "Can I connect my phone to Bluetooth?" "Yeah, sure," Mack said, turning on the dash screen. "I really hope you have a good playlist; it'd be a shame if I had to kick you out in the middle of the street. Jasmine laughed and said, "Ha-ha, very funny. I hope you like rap because it's one of my favorite genres." Soon, the car was filled with Lil Baby lyrics and bass boosted sound. "Lil Baby is my favorite rapper," said Mack, yelling over the music. He rolled down the windows and turned the music and bass up louder and started singing along.

When they got to The Teen Bar, Mack and Jasmine walked in and got a table for two in the back corner, away from other people. After they ordered, Jasmine said "I don't really ever eat here, my team and I just come and grab drinks after games." "Yeah, my teammates and I come here after every game, sometimes we eat, sometimes we just grab drinks, but the food's great here. I don't know the chef, but he definitely needs a raise." They talked about basketball and school until the food arrived about 15 minutes later. Jasmine took one bite into her catfish po-boy sandwich and her eyes lit up immediately. "This is the best sandwich I've ever eaten," she said, devouring it. "I told you the food's amazing," Mack said, digging into his own sandwich. They finished up about 20 minutes later, and just sat at the table talking. They were just walking out the door when some of Jasmine's teammates made their way to the front door. They saw Jasmine with Mack, and immediately started taking pictures and giggling. Mack pulled Jasmine towards the truck quickly, where they both hopped in, and Mack took off out of the parking lot. "Why'd you leave so quickly?" Jasmine said. "One of the last things I need is word of my injury getting out to the public. No one knows except for you, my family, and the team. Once the press gets a hold of this, not to mention us dating, we'll have more attention on us than we need, especially while trying to finish our seasons strong." Jasmine thought for a minute, then said, "I guess you're right. I'm going to try and make sure they don't leak those pictures on social media." Jasmine pulled her phone out and started furiously typing, while Mack connected his own phone to the truck's Bluetooth and started playing his own playlist.

When they got back to Jasmine's house, Mack put the car in park and turned to her. "Were you able to stop them from posting the pictures?" he asked. "They had the pictures on their Instagram stories for about 15 minutes, so I don't know who saw them or screenshot them. They said they were sorry, and that they didn't know. I told them not to take pictures while you were injured, because it will put more media attention on you. They said they wouldn't. As for anyone who saw the pictures, we'll know if anyone important saw them in a minute. You need to be focused on resting up, and letting your team take care of the next two games, so you'll be ready for the tournament." "Aye, aye captain," Mack said as Jasmine got out of the car. He waited until she locked herself in and drove off. He drove slowly, thinking to himself. "The biggest difference between a star and a superstar is how they respond after time away from the court," he thought. "All I have to do is stay the course and play my game, everything else will

come in time."

Epilogue

Roars and cheers echoed throughout the gym as the Hillmore Wolves took the floor for the first game of the North Forest Invitational. Their rivals, the Pine Hill Hawks, a team from Southern Massachusetts, took the court opposite them, and the warmups began.

After about 3 minutes, the ref called the two captains to center court, Mack and the Pine Hill point guard met at mid court to go over the rules. After the ref explained the rules, the two players shook hands and went back to their benches. Coach White put out his starting five, and when the Hawks got onto the court, the ref tossed the ball into the air. Jackson and the Hawks' center jumped for the tip, and the game began.

www.ingramcontent.com/pod-product-compliance
Lightning Source LLC
Chambersburg PA
CBHW072011150726
47999CB00002B/606